W9-AXO-901

Kevin
and His Dad

Kevin
and His Dad

by Irene Smalls

Illustrated by Michael Hays

TeachingStrategies™ · Washington, DC

Also by Irene Smalls:

A Strawbeater's Thanksgiving

Because You're Lucky

*Irene Jennie and the
Christmas Masquerade*

Louise's Gift

Jonathan and His Mommy

Irene and the Big, Fine Nickel

KEVIN AND HIS DAD Text copyright © 1999 by Irene Smalls. Illustrations copyright © 1999 by Michael Hays. This edition published by Teaching Strategies, Inc. by arrangement with Little, Brown and Company, New York, NY. All rights reserved.

ISBN 978-1-60617-203-2

CPSIA tracking label information: RR Donnelley, Shenzhen, China
Date of Production: November 2012 Cohort: Batch 2
Printed and bound in China

4 5	14 13 12
Printing	Year Printed

THE LIBRARY OF CONGRESS HAS CATALOGED THE
LITTLE BROWN EDITION AS FOLLOWS:

Library of Congress Cataloging-in-Publication Data

Smalls-Hector, Irene
  Kevin and his dad / by Irene Smalls ; illustrated by Michael Hays. — 1st. ed.
     p.   cm,
  Summary: Kevin feels excitement, pride, pleasure, and love as he spends an entire day working and playing with his father.
  ISBN 978-0-316-79899-0
  [1. Fathers and sons — Fiction.   2. Stories in rhyme.]   I. Hays, Michael, ill.
II. Title.
PZ8.3.S636Ke   1999
[E] — dc20   96-34830

The illustrations for this book were painted in acrylics on gessoed linen canvas.
The text was set in Stone Serif, and the display type is Utopia.

For Kevin Logan
"I love you, black child"
I. S.

For Wesley, Carl, Muriel,
Simone, and Janelle
M. H.

On Saturday, with Mom away,
Dad and I work — then we play.

First we take the vacuum and railroad the rugs —
choo, choo, coming through!
I love cleaning up with you.

Then we clean, clean, clean the windows,
wipe, wipe, wash them right.
My dad shines in the windows' light.

Next we pitch, pitch, pitch the papers,
fold, fold, fold the funnies,
basket, basket, basket the books,
tidy, tidy, tidy the toys.

We hang, hang, hang the hats,
catch, catch, catch the cobwebs.
We even dust, dust, dust the dog!

"I see a spot," Dad says as he touches my face
and rubs my hair all over the place.

Dad tells a joke and I start to giggle,
and I laugh and laugh until I wiggle.

We stop and take a little rest.
Being with my dad is really the best.

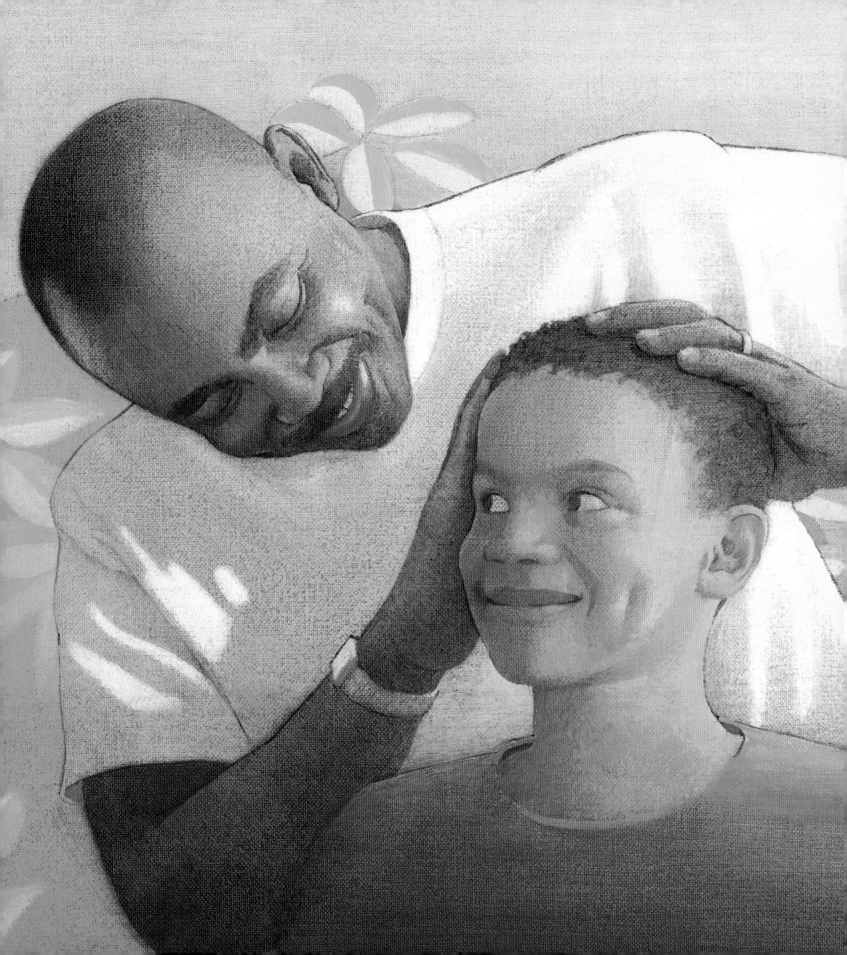

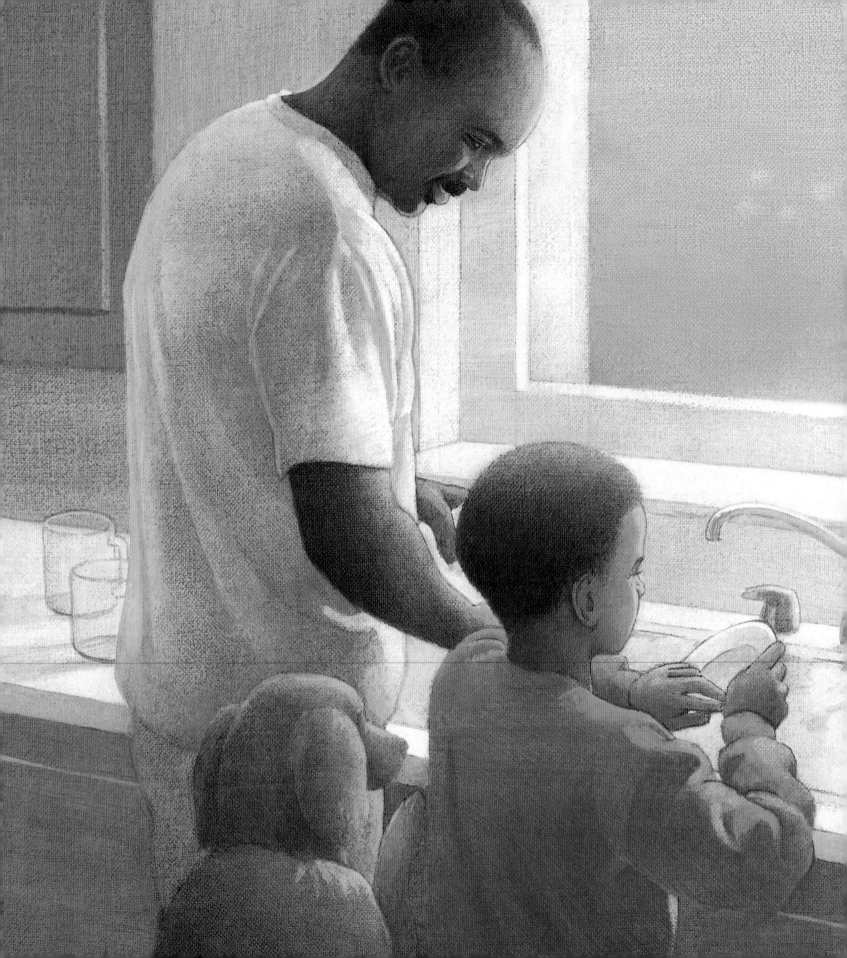

Next we fix, fix, fix the faucets,
squeeze, squeeze, squeeze the soap,
dunk, dunk, dunk the dishes.

We clean, clean, clean the clothes.
Hurry, hurry, hurry — shake a leg.
Last one done is a rotten egg!

After all, all, all is done —
pitching the papers,
folding the funnies,
basketing the books,
tidying the toys,
hanging the hats,
catching the cobwebs,
dusting the dog,
fixing the faucets,
squeezing the soap,
dunking the dishes,
cleaning the clothes . . .

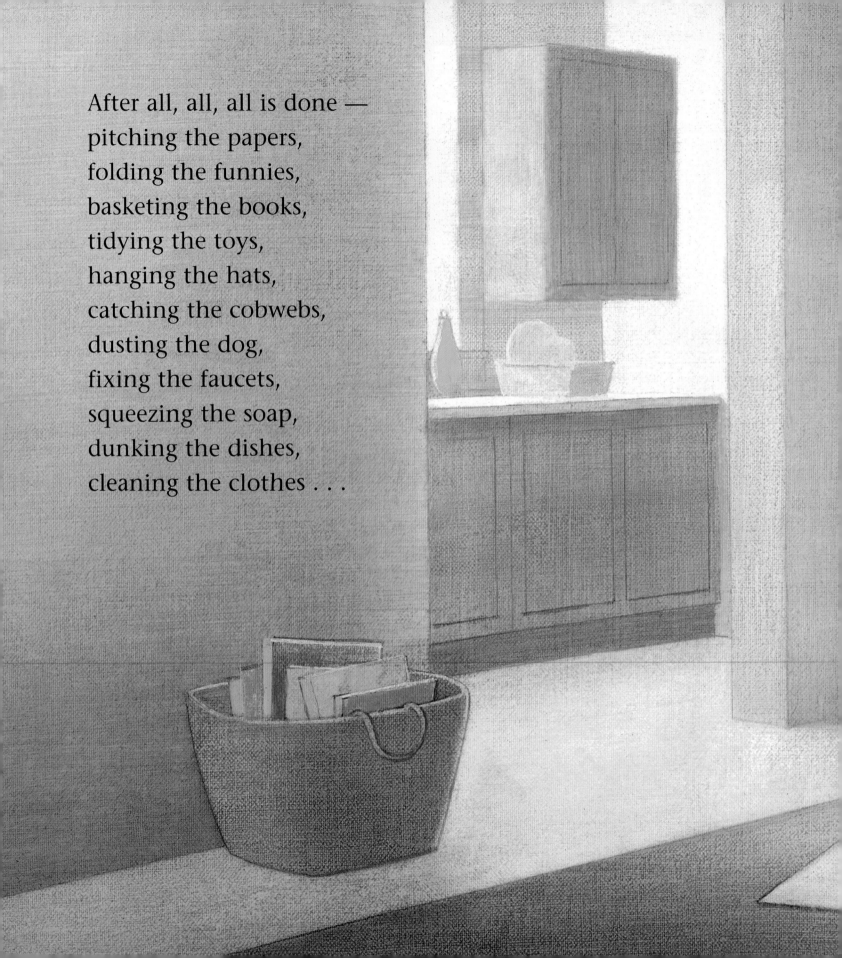

After all that is done,
Dad and I go out and have even more fun —
fast fun, funny fun, fat fun.

I get a bat while Dad grabs a mitt,
and we go to the park to see how many balls I can hit.

Then to the movies for an action flick —
there are two playing, so Dad lets me pick!

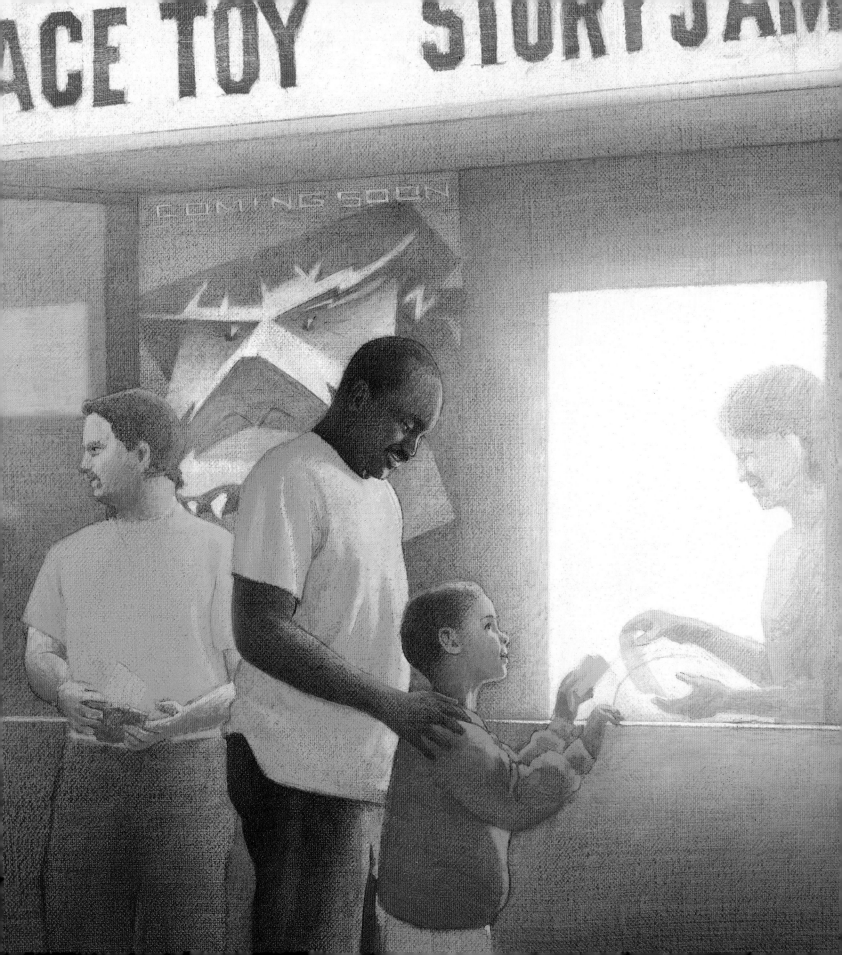

After the movies, we stop for a snack.
Before we know it, it's time to head back.

First we run, run, run a race
and dance, dance, dance all over the place.

Time goes so fast, so very, very fast;
I wish today could last and last and last.

P-N-BUY

CIGARETTES   BREAD   DAIRY PRODUCTS   D

Super
Low
P

MILK
$2.

A GRADE
OR 2%

Dad takes my hand and slows down.
I understand, and we walk through town.

It's a long, long walk.
We have a quiet talk and smile.

I love being with my dad;
he's the best friend a guy ever had.